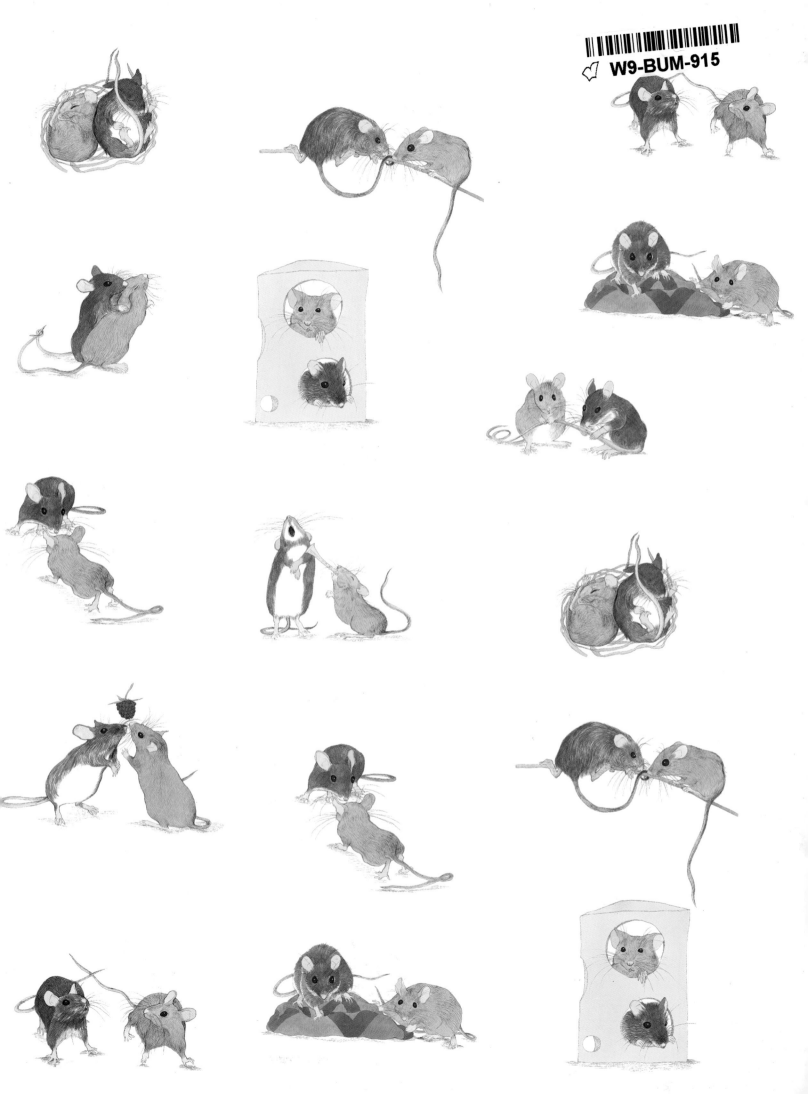

Lindsay Barrett George

INSIDE MOUSE, OUTSIDE MOUSE

Greenwillow Books, *An Imprint of* HarperCollinsPublishers

Inside my house
there is a mouse,

Outside my house
there is a mouse,

who sleeps in a clock.

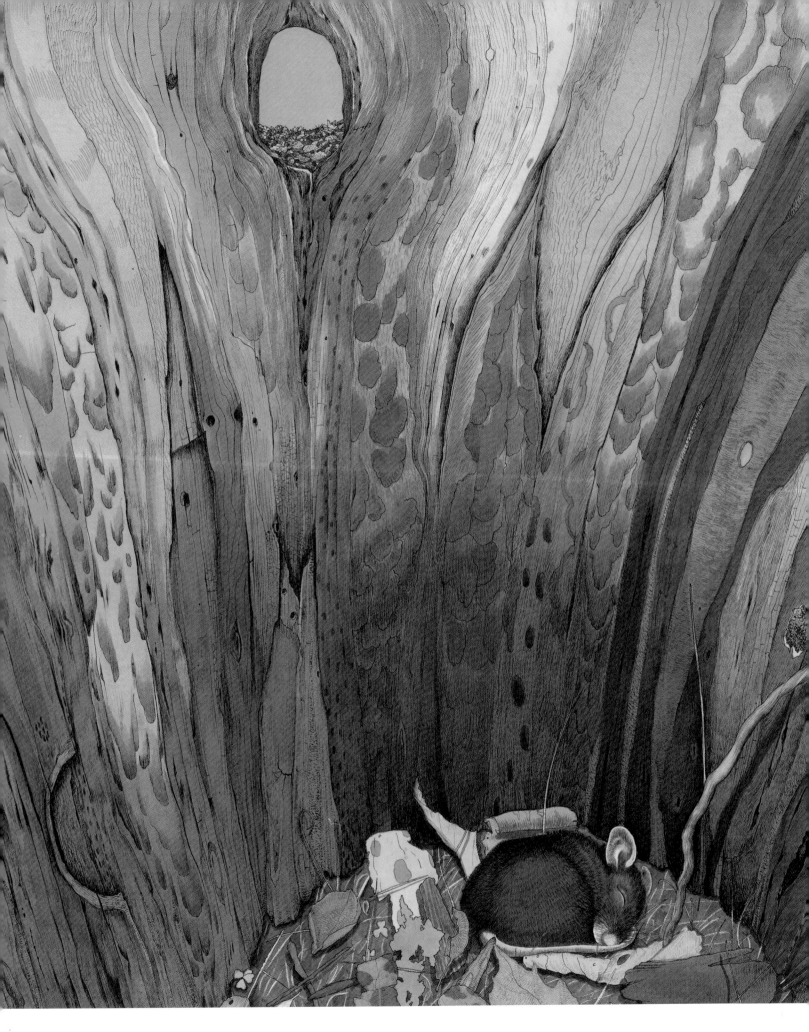

who sleeps in a stump.

The mouse ran down the wall,

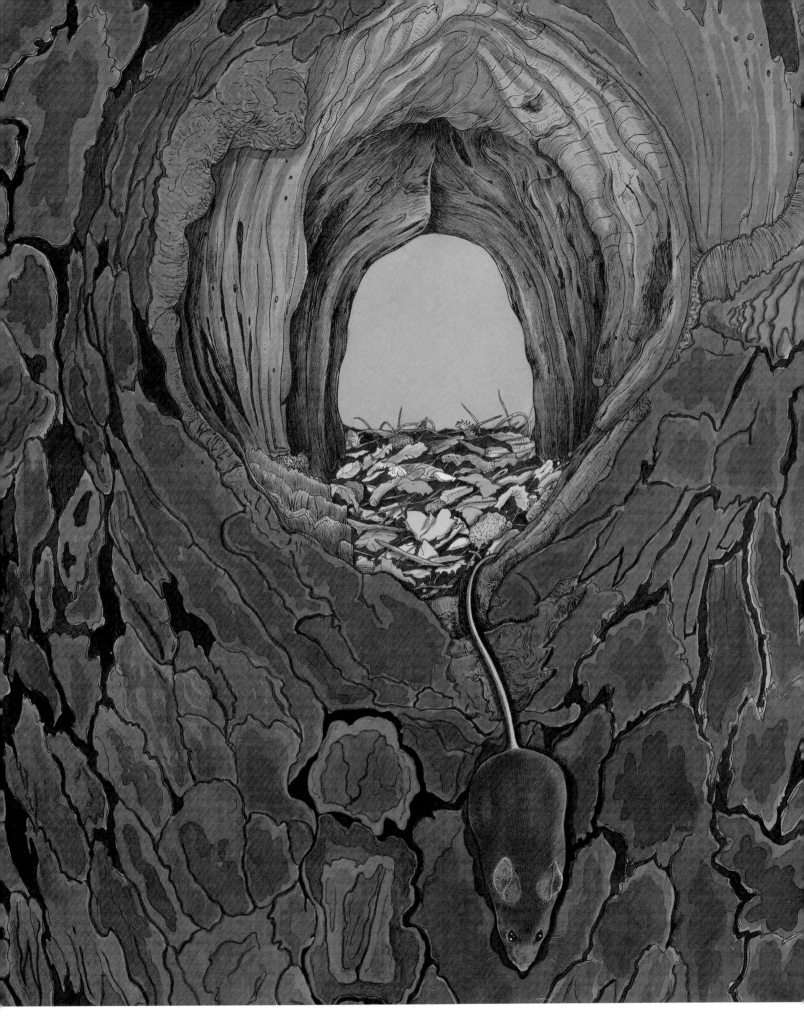

The mouse ran down the stump,

across the rug,

across the ground,

under the table, next to the cat.

under the bush, next to the hare.

He ran up the chair,

He ran up the wall,

in front of the dog,

in front of the squirrel,

into the can and out of the can.

into the can and out of the can.

He ran behind the book,

He ran behind the bird,

between the socks,

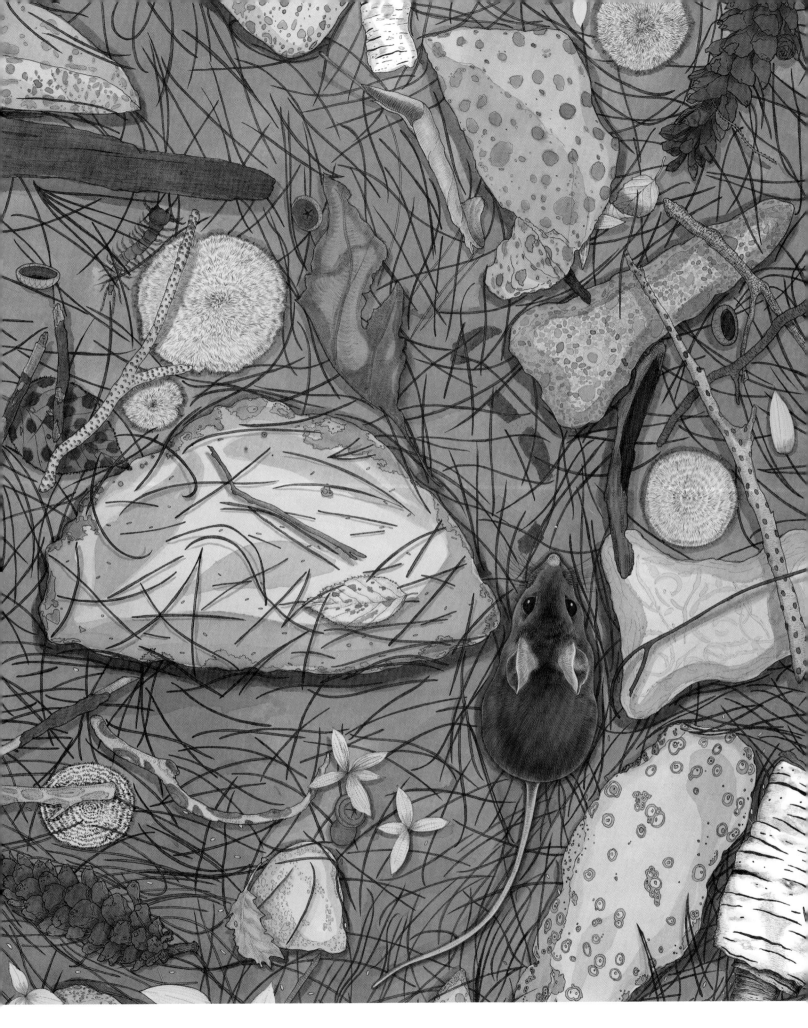

between the rocks,

below the spider, and over the ball.

below the spider, and over the stone.

He ran through the hole,

He ran through the hole,

along the bat,

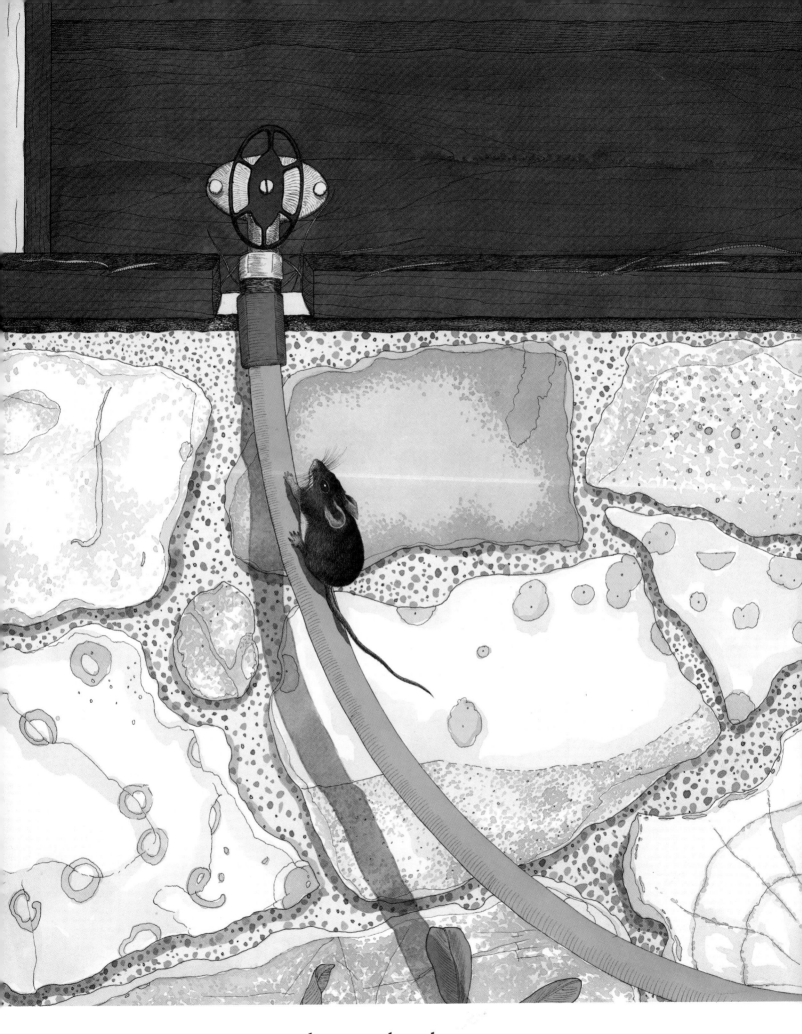

along the hose,

around the flowers, and stopped . . .

around the flowers, and stopped . . .

to look outside my house.

to look inside my house.

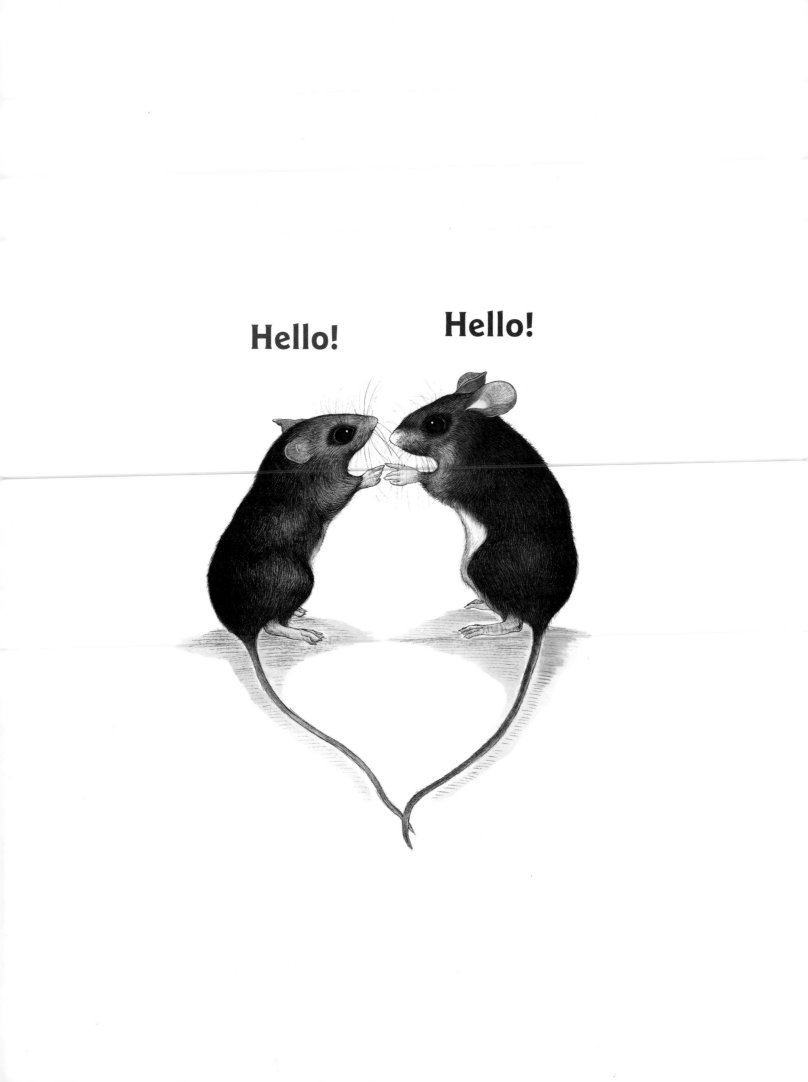

For Virginia
Thank you for giving me my voice.

—L. B. G.

Inside Mouse, Outside Mouse. Copyright © 2004 by Lindsay Barrett George. All rights reserved. www.harperchildrens.com.
Gouache paints were used to prepare the full-color art. The text of this book is set in GoudySans. Manufactured in China by South China Printing Company Ltd.

Library of Congress Cataloging-in-Publication Data. George, Lindsay Barrett. Inside mouse, outside mouse / by Lindsay Barrett George. p. cm. "Greenwillow Books."
Summary: Two mice, one who sleeps inside the house in a clock and one who sleeps outside the house in a stump, follow complicated but strangely parallel paths and meet each other at a window. ISBN 0-06-000466-5 (trade). ISBN 0-06-000467-3 (lib. bdg.). [1. Mice—Fiction.] I. Title. PZ7.G29334Im 2004 [E]—dc21 2003048497

1 2 3 4 5 6 7 8 9 10   First Edition

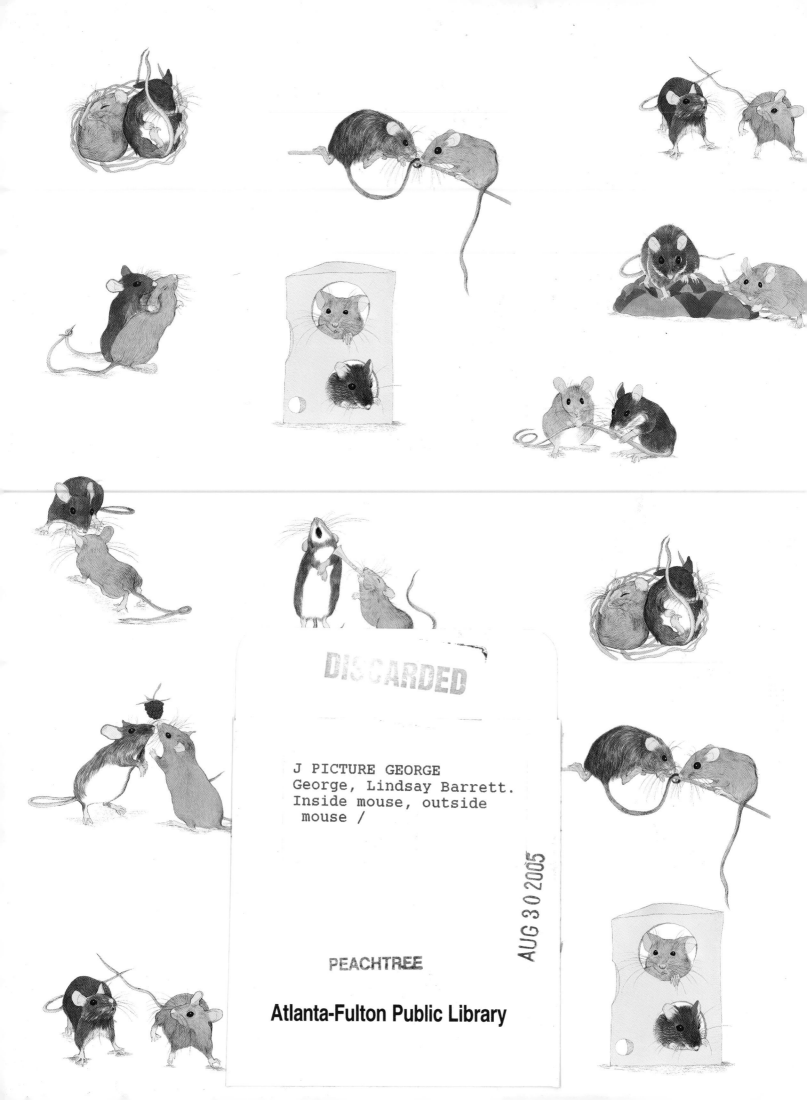